CHRISTMAS IN MY SOUL

Robin —

Merry Christmas

Barbara
2001

PETERSON'S

MAGAZINE

"HARK! THE HERALD ANGELS SING"

1881

CHRISTMAS IN MY SOUL

Edited and with an Introduction by

JOE WHEELER

Doubleday

New York London Toronto Sydney Auckland

PUBLISHED BY DOUBLEDAY
a division of Random House, Inc.
1540 Broadway, New York, New York 10036

DOUBLEDAY and the portrayal of an anchor with a
dolphin are registered trademarks of Doubleday,
a division of Random House, Inc.

Book design by Dana Leigh Treglia

Woodcut illustrations from the library of Joe Wheeler

Library of Congress Cataloging-in-Publication Data

Christmas in my soul / [edited by] Joe Wheeler—1st ed.
p.   cm.
Contents: Why the minister did not resign—Christmas
in Tin Can Valley—With a star on top / Margaret E.
Sangster, Jr.—Merry "little Christmas" / Agnes Sligh
Turnbull—The invisible Christmas trees / William
Barthel—A Christmas miracle / Kathleen R. Ruckman.
1. Christmas stories, American. 2. Christian fiction,
American. I. Wheeler, Joe L., 1936–
PS648.C45 C448 2000
813'.0108334—dc21
99-087932

ISBN 0-385-49859-4

Acknowledgments

Introduction: "From St. Nicholas to Santa Claus," by Joe Wheeler. Copyright © 1997 (revised 2000). Printed by permission of the author.

"Why the Minister Did Not Resign." Author and original source unknown. If anyone can provide knowledge of authorship, origin, and first publication of this old story, please relay this information to Joe Wheeler, care of Doubleday Religion Department.

"Christmas in Tin Can Valley." Author and original source unknown. If anyone can provide knowledge of authorship, origin, and first publication source of this old story, please relay this information to Joe Wheeler, care of Doubleday Religion Department.

Contents

CHRISTMAS IN

MY SOUL

INTRODUCTION

....

From St. Nicholas

to Santa Claus

All my life, I've wondered: *How in the world does one get from St. Nicholas to Santa Claus? And for that matter, who was St. Nicholas, and why do we still remember him today?* At last, with this introduction, I had an excuse to track down the answers. What I found out sheds a different light on today's plump, red-nosed, white-bearded man in red.

St. Nicholas himself is so be clouded in myth that it is almost impossible to separate fact from fiction. What is clear, however, is that he is one of the dominant figures of the last 1,600 years—and each age has found it necessary to reinvent him.

More than any other religious figure since the time of Christ, St. Nicholas has represented an ideal of goodness. For us, it is more important to discover how St. Nicholas has been *perceived* over the centuries than to know who he really *was*; especially since the real St. Nicholas is lost in the sands of time.

WHAT WE KNOW FOR CERTAIN

But first, let's start with what we *do* know for certain. In a word, the answer is "nothing."

WHAT SCHOLARS BELIEVE

Second, let's summarize what scholars *believe* to be true—even this is sketchy at best.

St. Nicholas was apparently born around A.D. 280 in

Patara, Lycia (kind of an oriental Switzerland, in modern-day Turkey). The apostle Paul knew Lycia well and converted many to Christianity here. His parents were rather wealthy devout Christians, and his uncle was a bishop in the church. As a child, Nicholas was precocious and grew up deeply religious, but his parents died in a plague epidemic. Later, upon the death of the incumbent bishop, Nicholas was ordained Bishop of Myra.

When Diocletian decreed that Christian churches be destroyed, their books burned, and all civil liberties taken away in the year 303, Nicholas was imprisoned because of his faith and tortured. Later, Nicholas was supposedly one of the 318 bishops called by Constantine to the famous Council of Nicaea (May 20 to July 25, 325). Nicholas died on December 6, 341. December 6 henceforth became St. Nicholas Day.

TRUTH, LEGEND, SPECULATION

Third, let's turn now to a hash of truth, legend, and speculation—out of which was forged the cult of St. Nicholas—fascinating ingredients for mythhood, all.

Over time, Nicholas's mother was portrayed as an infertile woman, thus a condition of his birth was that he be consecrated to a priestly ministry. The baby Nicholas was so precocious that he stood up in his bathtub almost as soon as he was born and he didn't demand his mother's breast on fast days—Wednesdays, Fridays—except after sunset. This spiritual precociousness continued through his growing-up years: being ordained at only nineteen (no doubt through the good offices of his uncle, who as bishop of a nearby bishopric, was his spiritual mentor).

Out of the goodness of his heart, and drawing upon the wealth of his estate, nineteen-year-old Nicholas secretly supplied his neighbor with the dowry money needed to arrange marriages for his three daughters. In this selfless way, he saved these women from almost certain lives of slavery or prostitution.

While on a pilgrimage to holy places, he predicted that God would miraculously save the ship despite a severe storm. During that trip, Nicholas brought a seaman back to life after a tragic fall from high on the mast. Other miracles attributed to Nicholas after he became Bishop of Myra include saving his people from starvation in a famine and reversing a cannibal's gruesome act by bringing three boys back to life and restoring them to their mother. Later, he intervened on behalf of three young men unjustly condemned to death, on the basis of perjurious charges, by a crooked judge. He then did the same for three officers of the Emperor Constantine, who found themselves in the same straights; only this time he appeared in the same dream experienced by the Emperor and his imperial Chancellor Evlavios.

At the pivotal Council of Nicaea, Nicholas was a champion of goodness in the theological power struggle between the Donatists and the Arians. When it came to conflicts with pagan religions, such as the cult of Artemis (or Diana), Nicholas waged a lifelong war against them and their temples.

This is about all we know about the "real-life" Nicholas. From these incidents the legend of St. Nicholas and all his spiritual and secular godchildren was built.

AND EACH AGE
REINVENTED HIM

From all appearances, the good bishop was not widely known in his time—in fact, he was not even mentioned by name in historical accounts of the famed Council of Nicaea. His world was that of Myra, in Asia Minor. But, after his death, stories of his kindness and his unwavering faith, and gradually over time the miracles associated with Nicholas, made him legendary in Myra. Complicating things even more was the fact that in the sixth century there was another Nicholas, Abbot of the Zion Monastery near Myra (later becoming Bishop of Pinara). He was a great traveler, and inevitably some of his achievements and exploits were folded into the St. Nicholas story.

In a world where the spirit realm featured prominently, for good or evil, early Christians gradually developed a mythology of devout and principled men and women, with whom Christians could identify. In Nicholas of Myra they found an ideal candidate. His mystique grew to such an extent that in the eleventh century zealous Christians abducted his remains from the Myra Cathedral, ostensibly to save them from the Saracens, and took them to Bari, Italy. Over that site, Pope Urban II built a great basilica.

A century before, in the year 911, Prince Oleg of the Russian principality of Kiev signed a treaty of friendship with the Byzantine rulers. In addition to sealing the treaty through marriages, they exchanged precious relics, among which were some of Nicholas's. Through Kiev, St. Nicholas entered Mother Russia, eventually becoming one of her patron saints, his name selected for several emperors.

In the twelfth- and thirteenth-century Catholic world, St. Nicholas ranked third only to Christ and the Virgin Mary as a venerated saint. His wide appeal led to all sorts of people taking him as their patron saint— seamen, children, marriageable daughters, the falsely accused, endangered travelers, farmers, bankers, pawn-brokers, traveling students, barren wives, pirating vandals, even thieves. The fighting bishop, the most human of all saints, became the patron saint of almost *everybody*.

Many of the medieval morality plays had to do with the life and ministry of St. Nicholas. Through these early dramas, simplistic and filled with raucous humor and buffoonery, the pious side of St. Nicholas gave way to one of at least slight humor. These plays were the real antecedents of today's short stories, novels, dramas, and the media darling we know as Santa. Artists in every age painted him. In the process, he took on certain stereotyped features—episcopal habit, mitre, cope, crozier, staff, book, and either three balls or three purses (for the three sisters and the three unjustly accused men he saved). Thanks to the Medici of Florence, the symbol of the three balls went global, as the symbol for financial transactions based on mutual trust; who better than St. Nicholas to represent unshakable trustworthiness (even though today's pawnshops fail to inspire the same confidence)?

Dutch master Jan Steen captured his country's patron saint in what can be described as the quintessential portrait of St. Nicholas. In the painting, a family of ten animate their anticipation of St. Nicholas. Surrounded by father, mother, grandmother, and six siblings, the oldest boy is pointing out, under the chimney place mantel, where St. Nicholas's presents are to come down— good children receiving sweets and toys, bad children bundles of switches.

So December 6, the day he died, came to be known as St. Nicholas Day. In many parts of Europe, even today, St. Nicholas Day remains the happiest day of the year for children. Shops are full of biscuits, gingerbread (many shaped like St. Nick), sugar images, toys, etc. On the Eve of St. Nicholas, St. Nicholas look-alikes, complete with mitre and staff, enquire about children's behavior, and, if good, pronounce a benediction and promise an appropriate reward the following day. Before they go to bed, children put out their shoes, with hay, straw, or a carrot for St. Nicholas's horse or donkey. When they awake on St. Nicholas Day, if they have been good, the fodder is gone and sweets and toys are there in their place; if bad, the fodder is left untouched and a rod or switches are left to encourage better behavior in the future. In Germanic countries, St. Nicholas, attired as a bishop, is impressive indeed: gray-haired with a flowing beard, gold-broidered cape, glittering mitre, and pastoral staff—riding a big white horse and followed by such fearsome creatures as a Pelsnickel, Black Peter, or Klaubauf, all serving as the punishers of bad children; and those who know their catechism are rewarded by another attendant who passes out candies, cookies, and other goodies.

Ironically, however anti-Catholic they may have been, leaders of the Protestant Reformation could not eradicate St. Nicholas from Europe. Eventually, they took the route of "If you can't beat 'em, join 'em" and gradually embraced this irresistible saint.

ST. NICHOLAS COMES
TO AMERICA

A good share of the Europeans who resettled in America brought the traditions of St. Nicholas with them. By now, some artists depicted him with a reindeer instead of a horse—sometimes both. Up to the early nineteenth century, however, St. Nicholas was almost invariably perceived in a spiritual rather than a secular light, hence St. Nicholas Day meshed well with the twenty-four days of Advent season.

In America, St. Nicholas became Santa Claus rather quickly and easily. Thanks to Dutch settlers in New York, who called St. Nicholas "Sinta Claes," his name made the transition. Eventually, in 1810, John Pintard, founder of the New-York Historical Society and a key figure in making Washington's birthday and the Fourth of July national holidays, organized a St. Nicholas celebration. One year before, Washington Irving was nominated for membership in the New-York Historical Society.

Now came the one, two, three, punch that transformed St. Nicholas into Santa Claus. First and foremost, Washington Irving (1783–1859) created the mythological story for the change in his hilarious spoof, *A History of New York from the Beginning of the World to the End of the Dutch Dynasty* by "Diedrich Knickerbocker," originally published in 1809. Irving's genius was such that readers in the New, as well as the Old, World found the mock epic so convincing that it was almost impossible for them to separate fact from fiction. Here a plump, merry St. Nicholas/Santa Claus takes the stage no less than twenty-five times in the work, including the memorable scene where he flies his gift-laden wagon over treetops, stops for a rest in the forest to smoke his pipe, then lays his finger beside his nose before mounting his wagon once more and disappearing over the trees.

Irving's story soon sparked an important elaboration, by the distinguished clergyman Dr. Clement Clarke Moore (1779–1863), a Hebrew scholar at General Theological Seminary, in New York City. As Christmas 1822 approached, Dr. Moore, an accomplished poet, decided to compose a present for his children. Suddenly, the concept came to him: to bring to life via poetry Irving's unique depiction of St. Nicholas. Always before, St. Nicholas had been depicted as lanky, but Irving's version of a jolly fat man opened the door for Moore to elaborate and embellish a new St. Nicholas for his children that evening of December 23, 1822, when he read "A Visit from St. Nicholas." That might have been the end of it had not a lady visitor been there that night; she begged a copy and had it published anonymously in the *Sentinel* of Troy, New York, at Christmastime 1823.

Commonly known as "'Twas the night before Christmas," Moore's creation has become *the* St. Nicholas story. Now it is hard to think of Christmas without conjuring up images of stockings "hung by the fire with care," "visions of sugar-plums" dancing in the children's heads, "a miniature sleigh and eight tiny reindeer," and St. Nicholas as "a right jolly old elf."

But Moore's poem by itself would quite possibly not have survived without the help of German-born cartoonist Thomas Nast (1840–1902). Through his drawings, Nast made his mark in the political arena, toppling New York's corrupt Boss Tweed and Tammany Hall and creating the donkey symbol for the Democratic Party and elephant for the Republican Party. Starting in the early 1860s, Nast began a series of woodcut illustrations depicting St. Nicholas/Santa Claus for the Christmas issues of *Harpers Illustrated Monthly Magazines*. He based the drawings on Irving's story, Moore's poem, and his own Germanic cultural heritage. These woodcut illustrations circulated *everywhere*—not only in the magazine, but as large prints, gift cards, and postcards as well.

The most widely publicized and circulated Christmas editorial of all time was written anonymously by Frances Pharcellus Church and published by *The New York Sun* on September 21, 1897. An eight-year-old girl, Virginia O'Hanlon, who had always believed in the existence of Santa Claus (for so Americans were then calling St. Nicholas), found her beliefs challenged by children she knew. When even her father's answers seemed evasive, she turned to the family court of last resort, the *Sun* "Question and Answer" column; "for Father has always said, 'If you see it in the *Sun*, it's so.'"

After what probably seemed like an eternity to little Virginia, she got her answer in an editorial by Frances Pharcellus Church titled, "Yes, Virginia, There Is a Santa Claus!" After initial hesitation, the cynical, crusty editor, a former Civil War correspondent with no children of his own, penned a remarkable editorial arguing unequivocally that Santa Claus indeed exists. It went *everywhere* and did much to validate the place of Santa Claus/St. Nicholas in American culture.

Finally, the person who put the exclamation point on the modern Santa, Haddon Sundblom, did so through his depictions of Santa Claus on Coca-Cola ads. Splendidly illustrated and reproduced by the millions, these pictures brought the 1,600-year development of the St. Nicholas image to its current state.

SO WHAT DOES IT
ALL MEAN?

As we have already noted, each age has reinvented St. Nicholas in order to adapt him to its unique needs. When Christianity was new and education almost nonexistent, a deeply spiritual and mystical depiction was natural. That state of affairs continued for close to a millennium, through the Crusades and the great Age of Faith that spawned Europe's soaring Gothic cathedrals.

Along with the Renaissance, the Reformation, the Enlightenment, on up to the present, we have adapted St. Nicholas to our world and our needs. In time, he became ecumenicized, the secular co-opted the sacred, and he who was St. Nicholas was remade in the image of Santa

Claus. Still a good, kind figure, yes. In fact, about as benign a popular image as one could get.

Looking back on my own life, I note that my conservative minister father, who dressed up in a Santa suit every Christmas, yet simultaneously managed to keep our Christmases spiritual, was able to wed the best of the spiritual and secular worlds—for we do have to coexist in both.

But . . . Santa Claus alone, or even St. Nicholas alone, without the life, crucifixion, death, and resurrection of our Lord, is a travesty on what Christmas is all about! Christ *is* indeed, and must remain, the central core, the reason behind the season.

....

NOTE: I am deeply indebted to Martin Ebon's fascinating *St. Nicholas: Life and Legend* (Harper & Row, 1975), which has been invaluable in helping me grasp the significance of the St. Nicholas Phenomenon. I also found Eugene R. Whitmore's *St. Nicholas, Bishop of Myra* (private printing, 1944) and Clement A. Miles's *Christmas in Ritual and Tradition, Christian and Pagan* (T. Fisher Unwin, London, 1912, 1968) to be helpful.

ABOUT THIS COLLECTION

While this is the first yearly *Christmas in My Soul* collection, it is the fifth annual collection by Doubleday, the first four being titled *Christmas in My Heart*. Thus new readers will wish to pick up copies of the earlier collections. The now bestselling *Christmas in My Heart* series had its beginning in 1992, that paperback collection published by Review and Herald Publishing Association. Of the six authors presented in this collection, one will already be familiar to our readers, Margaret E. Sangster, Jr. ("The Lonely Tree," "The Littlest Orphan and the Christ Baby"), in the second and third *Christmas in My Heart* treasuries.

CODA

Virtually every day's mail brings welcome correspondence from you. Many of your letters are testimonials to the power of certain stories; virtually *all* of them express gratitude for the series. Others include favorite stories for possible inclusion down the line (some of them Christmas-related and others tying in with other genre collections we are working on). These letters from you not only brighten each day for us, but help to provide the stories that make possible future story anthologies.

May the good Lord bless and guide each of you.

You may contact me at the following address:
Joe Wheeler, Ph.D.
c/o Doubleday Religion Department
1540 Broadway
New York, New York 10036

WHY THE MINISTER DID NOT RESIGN

....

Author Unknown

One of the first Christmas stories I can remember my mother reciting—almost all were by memory—is this one. My mother puts all of herself into her recitations: laughing in hilarious passages and crying in moving ones. This is one of her tearjerkers: to the best of my knowledge, she never got through this Hatfield-McCoyish tale dry-eyed. Neither did her audiences.

He waited until she put the baby down, then he met her in the middle of the room and said it.

"I shall do it next Sabbath, Rebekah."

"O Julius, not NEXT Sabbath!" she cried out in dismay. "Why, next Sabbath is Christmas, Julius!"

Julius Taft's smooth-shaven lips curled into a smile.

"Well, why not, little woman? It would be a new way to celebrate Christmas. Everyone likes a 'new way.' The holly and the carols are so old!"

"Julius!"

"Forgive me, dear; but my heart is bitter. I cannot bear it any longer. I shall do it next week, Rebekah."

"But afterward, Julius?"

The mother's eyes wandered to the row of little chairs against the wall, each with its neatly folded little clothes. There were three little chairs and the baby's crib. Afterward, what about those? They argued mutely against this thing.

"Afterward, I'll dig ditches to earn bread for the babies—don't worry, little mother!" He laughed unsteadily. Then he drew her down with him on the sofa.

"Let's have it out, dear. I've borne it alone as long as I can."

"Alone!" she scolded softly. "Julius Taft, you know I've been bearing it with you!"

"I know it, dear; but we've both kept still. Now let's talk it out. It's no use beating about the bush, Rebekah, I've got it to do."

"O Julius, if we could only peacemake!" she wailed.

"But we can't—not even the minister's little peacemaker wife. They won't let us do it—they'd rather wrangle."

She put her hand across his lips to stifle the ugly word; but she knew it applied.

"They don't realize, Julius. If Mrs. Cain and Mrs. Drinkwater would only realize! They influence all the rest. Everyone would make up, if they would. They're the ones to peacemake, Julius."

"Yes, but Drinkwaters and Cains won't 'peacemake'—you can't make oil and water unite. There was a grudge between them three generations ago, and it's descending. I can't see any way out of it."

"But on Christmas, Julius! 'Peace on earth, good will to men,'" Rebekah Taft murmured softly. The minister sighed heavily.

"There isn't any 'peace, good will' in the Saxon church, Rebekah. It won't be any special service. It will be just like all the other services, only the minister will resign."

"But he will preach a Christmas sermon, Julius? Tell me he will!" pleaded the minister's little peacemaker wife.

"Yes, dear, he will preach a Christmas sermon to please his little wife."

They sat quite silent awhile. The sleeping baby nestled and threw out a small pink and white hand aimlessly. The clock on the painted mantel said, "Bedtime, bedtime, bedtime!" with monotonous repetition.

They were both very tired, but they still sat side by side on the hard little sofa, thinking the same sorrowful thoughts. It was the wife who first broke the silence.

"Dear, there are so many things to think about," she whispered.

He smiled down at her from his superior height.

"Four things," he counted on his fingers. "Katie, Julius Junior, Hop-o'-My-Thumb, and the baby!"

"Yes, I meant the children. If you—"

Julius Taft was big and broad-shouldered. He drew himself up and faced her. His lean, good face was the face of a man who would create the opportunity that he could not find ready to his hand.

"Did the children's mother think all I could do was to preach?" he cried gaily. He could not bear the worry in her dear face. "She's forgotten I blew the bellows in my father's smithy. I can blow them again! I can find good, honest work in God's world, dear heart, never fear, and it will be infinitely better than preaching to a divided people."

"Yes, it will be better," she agreed; and then they listened to the clock.

The little church at Saxon had its feud. It had brought it a certain kind of fame in all the countryside. Other churches pointed to it with indulgent pity. Strangers over in Krell and Dennistown were regaled with entertaining accounts of how the Saxon congregation was divided by the broad aisle into two hostile factions, and no man stepped across.

"It's the dead line," chuckled the Krell newsmonger in chief. "No one but the minister dares go across! Those for the Cain side sit on one side of the aisle, and those for the Drinkwater side sit on the other. The gallery is reserved for neutrals, but it's always empty! They make it terribly hard for their parson over there in Saxon."

The Krell newspaper was right. It *was* terribly hard for the minister at Saxon. For eight years he and his gentle little wife had struggled to calm the troubled waters, but still they flowed on turbulently. Still there was discord, whichever way one turned. Another congregation might have separated farther than a broad aisle's width long ago, and worshipped in two churches instead of one. But the Saxon congregation had its own way of doing things. Its founders had been original, and generation upon generation had inherited the trait.

Midway in the week preceding Christmas, Julius Taft came to the little parsonage nursery, with signals of fresh distress plainly hoisted.

"Well?"

Rebekah Taft stopped rocking and waited. The baby in her arms lurched joyously toward the tall figure.

"Well, Julius?"

"Please, ma'am, may I come in and grumble? I'm 'that' full I can't hold in! Here, give me the youngster. What do you suppose has happened now, little woman?"

"The church has blown up!" guessed Rebekah.

"Not yet, but the fuse is lighted. I've just found out about the Christmas music. I hoped they would not have any."

"O Julius, so did I! It will be sure to make trouble."

"It's made it already. That's IT! I've just found out that Mrs. Cain is drilling her little Lethia to sing a carol; you know she has a beautiful little voice."

"Yes, oh, yes, as clear as a bird's. Why won't it be beautiful to have her sing, Julius?"

"Because Mrs. Drinkwater is drilling Gerry to sing," the minister said dryly.

"Oh!"

"And it won't be a duet, little woman."

They both laughed, and the shrill crow of the baby chimed in. Only the baby's laugh was mirthful. The minister's worn face sobered quickly.

"I don't know how it will come out," he sighed. "They are both very determined, and the hostile feeling is so strong. I wish it might have held off a little longer—till you and I got back to the smithy, dear!"

....

O ut in the leafless orchard, back of the parsonage, a little group of children was collected together on a mild December afternoon. The two factions that pertained among their elders were distinctly visible there. Two well-defined groups stood aloof, eyeing each other with family scorn. Between the two groups, mid-way, the minister's two little children stood, apparently in a conciliatory mood.

"Let's play meeting," suggested Julius Junior, the paternal mantle on his small, square shoulders. "I'll preach."

"Oh, yes, do let's!—we're so sick of playing battle," urged Kathie eagerly. Battle was the favorite play, pre-sumably on account of the excellent opportunities it of-fered the opposing parties.

"Sit down by the big log—there's a good place. This rock's my pulpit," bustled the little minister, importantly, and the children scurried into place. It was noteworthy that the broad trunk of the old fallen tree set apart the rival factions. On each side squatted the divided congre-gation. Julius Junior's little lean brown face assumed a serious expression. He stood awhile in deep thought. Then his face brightened.

"I know! I'll preach you a Christmas sermon!" he cried softly. "That will be very ap-pro-perate, because Sabbath is Christmas, you know. Now, I'll begin. My text today is—is—I know! 'Peace on earth, good will to men'—that's it—'Peace on earth, good will to men.'"

It was sunny and still in the orchard behind the parsonage. The rows of children's faces put on piety as a garment and were staidly solemn. The small minister's face was rapt. Suddenly a high, sweet voice interrupted.

"I'll sing the carols," it cried.

"No, I'LL sing 'em!"

"My mother's taught me how. I guess I'm the one that's going to sing 'em on Christmas!"

"I guess you aren't, Lethia Cain! I guess my mother's been teaching me."

"My mother says I'm going to sing 'em—so there, Gerry Drinkwater!"

"My mother says I'M going to—SO THERE!"

The small rivals glared at each other. A murmur of supporting wrath rose behind each. The little minister looked worried—the paternal mantle weighed heavily.

"Hush!" he cried earnestly, "we'll have congregational singing instead. Sit right down—I'm goin' to preach."

For a little while there was only the sound of his earnest voice in the snowy orchard, with the soft, sighing wind for its only accompaniment. He preached with deep fervor. Two tiny spots of color blossomed out in his cheeks as he went on.

" 'Peace on earth'—that means everybody's to

be friends with everybody else," he said. "Everybody's to be peaceful an' loving, an' kind, same's the Lord Jesus was. Do you s'pose He'd have sat on the same side of the broad aisle every single Sabbath that ever was? No, my friends, I'll tell you what the Lord would have done. He'd have sat on your side up to the sermon, Lethia, and then He'd have gone 'cross, tiptoe an' soft, in His beautiful white robe, an' sat on Gerry's side clear through to the benediction—just to make 'peace on earth.' Can't you most see Him sitting there—"

The minister's little brown face shone with a solemn light.

"Can't you see how peaceful He'd have looked, an' how lovin'-kind? An' then my father'd have asked Him to say the benediction, an' He'd have spread out His hands over us an' said, softly, 'Peace on earth, good will to men' an' that would have meant for us to love each other, an' sit together, and sing out o' the same hymn book."

It was quiet under the leafless apple trees. All the little faces were solemn. It was as if the white-robed Guest were among them, stepping across the dividing line, "tiptoe an' soft"—as if His hands were spread out over them in benediction.

" 'Peace on earth, good will to men.' "

The small faces gazed at each other solemnly. The little minister went on with staunch courage, his hands unconsciously extended.

"It would have meant to sing your Christmas carols out o' the same hymn book. Why don't you do it today, just as if He was here?"

He waited confidently, and not in vain. Two little figures, one at each end of the long log, stood up and began to sing. Gradually they drifted nearer until they stood side by side. Their high, childish voices blended sweetly.

....

Julius Taft worked on his Christmas sermon with a heavy heart. The war clouds seemed to be gathering ominously. Rumors of war crept in to him, in his quiet study.

"I don't know how it's coming out, little woman," he sighed. "I have done everything I can—I've been to see them both, those women. Both of them have their plans made unchangeably, and, if they collide, then—the crash."

"Yes, then the crash," sighed the minister's wife.

"I tried to persuade them both; you don't know how hard I worked, dear! But all the while I knew I was wasting time and might as well come home to my sermon. Now I am going to wait; but, remember, something will happen tomorrow. Rebekah—two things."

"Two, Julius?"

"Yes; the minister's resignation and the crash."

He laughed, but his pale face smote her, and she crept onto his knee, and laid her own pale face against his. Somewhere in the house they could hear children's happy voices. It helped them.

"They are dear children, Julius," the mother whispered.

"God bless them!" he said.

"Yes—oh, yes, God bless them! And He will, Julius. I think our boy will be a preacher."

"Then the Lord help him," the minister cried.

....

Christmas morning dawned clear, crisp, and beautiful. Chimes in the bell tower tolled out their Christmas music, but the little carolers at Saxon were missing when church time came. Their mothers searched for them vainly. But both children had disappeared at the close of Sabbath school. No one could find them.

The last bell rang, and in despair, each mother gave up the search and went to her seat alone. They were both fretted and disappointed, but were palpably relieved to discover that their losses were mutual.

In the minister's pew the minister's wife sat among her brood with gentle dignity.

Service began and went on a little monotonously. On both sides of the broad aisle there was evident keen disappointment, as though some anticipated relish had failed. Everyone had expected that something would happen. The absence of little Lethia Cain and Gerry Drinkwater dispelled the possibility.

The minister prayed in his earnest, direct way, and the opening hymn was announced. It was then that the something happened, after all. Suddenly, high, sweet music sounded in the people's ears— clear, high music, such as only the voices of little children can make. It came nearer—up the broad aisle! There were two voices. Two little children trudged up the aisle, hand in hand, singing a Christmas carol.

"'Al-le-lu-ia! Al-le-lu-ia! Peace, good will—on—earth,'" the childish voices sang. They filled the quiet church with clear melody. The people's listening faces softened and grew gentle. The two mothers leaned forward, breathlessly.

"'Al-le-lu-ia! Al-le-lu-ia!'" high and sweet, triumphant. "'Peace on earth, good will to men!'"

At the altar rail the same figures swung about, still singing. They stood there, hand in hand, till the carol ended. There were many stanzas, and they sang them all. At the end they walked gravely down the aisle and seated themselves each in the other's place, while the people stared.

Little Lethia Cain nestled down beside Mrs. Drinkwater and beamed up into her astonished face with a friendly smile.

"HE would have—the Lord—you know," she whispered.

And across the aisle, in the Cain pew, little Gerry Drinkwater snuggled down comfortably, with an audible sigh of relief.

"I'm glad THAT'S over!" he whispered distinctly. "We did it 'cause 'twas Christmas, and HE'D have liked to hear us singin' out of the same hymn book, you know.

That's why we've swapped places, too—to make 'peace on earth.' Don't you see?"

"Yes," whispered Mrs. Cain softly, "I see, Gerry." And she glanced across at the other mother with a little of Gerry's "peace on earth" in her softened face.

....

The sermon in the orchard has borne its fruit. The other sermon on Christmas morning was to bear fruit too, for the young minister preached as never before, and his congregation listened. The little children had led them—should they not follow?

The lines of patient worry in Rebekah Taft's face smoothed out one by one. A prescience of peace to come stole into her troubled heart and comforted it. Over the whole church brooded the Christmas spirit of love and peace and good fellowship.

And the minister did not resign.

CHRISTMAS IN

TIN CAN VALLEY

....

Author Unknown

*E*ver since my Christmas anthologies began, I have been urged to include this old story. Initially, I held back, thinking the story too simplistic and didactic. But the requests kept coming. Finally, I decided to reread it again to see if I could discover why this simple little story had such an amazing following, why it was so loved. I read it this time with no attempt to see if

it was worthy to be included because of its craftsman-
ship, merely to let it speak to me—or fail to do so.

This time, becoming as a little child myself, at last I
learned the secret of the story. If you, too, become as a
little child, you will also learn the secret.

....

t was the Yule season in Hollis Hollow, U.S.A. I
say U.S.A. because this story could happen in
almost any town of our country, yes, even here in this
city of ours. Ragged and dirty children, ragged and dirty
women, ragged and dirty men; careworn housewives and
mothers trying to make their poorly made shacks worthy
of the name "Home." Discouraged fathers trying to
provide for their families on the city's dumping grounds;
yes, large cities are familiar with the scene and it is not
uncommon to find back in the more remote sections of
the thriving town or village, places where filth and dirt
breed disease, crime, and pathetic conditions.

Tin Can Valley started as a rubbish heap, and not
long after the city started using Hollis Hollow as a dumping ground, the poorer element drifted in and sifted from
the rubbish such things that could be used for their phys-

ical substance and shelter. Crude shacks were made from store boxes and discarded sheets of tin; old stoves were patched and propped until they were able to give out a little warmth and heat for cooking; discarded bricks and stones were fashioned into crude fireplaces and chimneys; other bits of material considered useless in more prosperous sections of the city were eagerly seized by the inhabitants of Tin Can Valley and placed here and there, rigged up with boards, blocks, bricks, and sticks, until various pieces of furniture were peculiarly manufactured out of practically nothing.

Being a resident of Tin Can Valley was nothing of which to be proud, although their names were in the papers quite a bit: so many contagious diseases, so many criminal acts, and so many disturbances—but to extend a helping hand, to look upon these people with love as souls that God wanted in His kingdom, too, wasn't given much thought.

Now the Christmas Season was approaching. The stores temptingly displayed their gorgeous merchandise. Eyes grew large, ears opened wide, little minds were active, and imaginations were stretched to the widest possible extent as children watching and wondering eagerly anticipated the joys of Christmas morning, with that special toy all their own they had gazed at in the shop windows, or on the laden counters, or in the overflowing showrooms. The season was a time of joy for everyone—for everyone, that is, except for the people of Tin Can Valley. Little eyes were just as wide, ears could hear just as well, little minds were also active, and imaginations were plentiful, but there was no joy of anticipation. Tired mothers and downhearted fathers had brusquely informed their inquiring youngsters that gifts only came to those who were wealthy, those on the hill, and never-never to Tin Can Valley. Occasionally some well-meaning church society had sent a basket or two with food and a few discarded toys, but discarded things were so common among the wretched boys and girls that it was nothing to be excited about—nothing like they saw in the brilliantly lighted windows of the business section.

....

immie lived in Tin Can Valley. His was one of the store box shacks of one room. One small window let in a little light by day and an oil lamp gave a little light by night—that is, it did when Jimmie could sell a few papers or his mother could find work as an extra, washing dishes at a nearby restaurant, to buy oil with and then that was bought only after the other necessities were provided for first. Just like any other eight-year-old boy in the Valley, Jimmie was filled with the natural pep and vim of a growing boy.

One day a lady visited the little shack where Jimmie and his widowed mother lived. She smiled so sweetly and spoke so kindly that Jimmie wondered where she had come from. Surely not from the city. His little playmates had told him those people were all cross and mean. Finally he ventured the question, "Where did you come from?"

"Not far from here, son," she replied. "I came to help you people here in the Hollow."

"How?" This was something new to Jimmie. No one but Mother had ever offered to help him before.

"First, by telling you a beautiful story," she answered. Jimmie listened intently. This was so strange, so unreal, so impossible, and yet—why, this babe must have been born in a place something like Tin Can Valley, he decided. But this lady had said that wealthy men brought him pretty gifts because he was a king. After the lady had gone, the boy thought over and over the words she had spoken and that night Jimmie crept out under the stars and looked up into the heavens. It was bitterly cold, and he shivered as he drew his coat more closely about his thin body; not noting crunching steps in the crisp snow, as he gazed intently heavenward.

"Watcha doin', Jim?" a gruff voice spoke close to his ear as a figure halted near him.

"Lookin' fer the star," he answered.

"Hadn' oughta have any trouble. Plenty of 'em up there," the man replied.

"Not the star that showed where the baby was that night when Jesus was born," Jimmie answered.

"Better go in an' get warm," the neighbor advised and trudged on to his own little shack, but thinking—a baby born—in a manger—um—maybe there was something to Christmas after all. He remembered hearing the story when he was a boy, but he had forgotten about the real heart of the story. A pang shot through him as he opened the door. One time he had happiness when he knew and believed that story. Perhaps he could find it again.

I t was the day before Christmas. The lady again came to see Jimmie and his mother. And this time she invited them both to come to the mission that night. And such wonderful things she promised—lovely music and the Christmas story and gifts, real gifts for each of them! Oh! The joy of anticipation was known to Jimmie now. Jimmie clapped his hands with delight. "But won't you tell me about the baby again right now?" he entreated.

"It is because of him," she had finished after repeating the story, "that I am here now and that we are giving you gifts tonight, and he has told us to go tell others."

Jimmie had never seen anything so wonderful in his whole life. He and his mother sat very near the front. There was such beautiful music, "Joy to the World," and then a man arose and told them softly the story of Jesus. He could hear the soft strains of "O Little Town of Bethlehem." Why—remember that was the town where the baby was born; but the man was speaking again. He was telling the story all over again, only he didn't end with the wise men; he told how the baby grew into a little boy and became a man, and such wonderful things he did helping people, healing them when they were sick, and teaching them how to live. And then—Jimmie's eyes filled with tears—then some cruel men took him and killed him. But, the man was saying that this man, whom he called Jesus, had risen from his grave, and was at that very moment now living in Heaven. First dying and now living so that everyone— why, Jimmie thought, that means *me*—"could live with him forever more."

Jimmie hung on every word. At last the minister had finished and some other men were passing out baskets, baskets filled with good things to eat and a toy and candy for every boy and girl in the Valley. It was all so wonderful, and yet Jimmie kept thinking of the story. Quietly he slipped up to the minister and touched his coat sleeve. "Say, minister!" he exclaimed. "Did you say that baby died for people?"

The man looked down with kindly eyes at the up-turned face; "Yes, my boy."

"Then he died for me?"

"Yes, sonny."

"And I should tell others who don't know it, shouldn't I, 'cause the lady said that's why she told me the story?"

The man nodded and patted the boy's head. Then

Mother called, and soon Jimmie was nestling up against her in the mission truck as it carried its load back to the Valley.

....

Tin Can Valley was happier that Christmas Eve than it had ever been before, but Jimmie was happiest of all. There was a newfound peace and joy in his heart that only Christ could give. His heart was filled to overflowing and he repeated the story over and over to his careworn mother until she, too, caught a glimpse of the joy offered by the Savior.

Christmas morning was ushered in by a blustering wind, bearing upon its wings bits of stinging sleet and snow which, as the day lengthened, turned into a blinding blizzard. Jimmie was up at dawn, drawing on his thin coat and worn cap. He kissed his mother and darted out into the snow. At length he returned cold and shivering. But he was smiling and happy.

"My boy, where have you been?" his mother asked, drawing him toward the little stove that was struggling bravely to radiate a little heat.

"Telling all the folks in Tin Can Valley about Jesus."

The Christmas dinner was greatly enjoyed by Mother and son, and there was enough food given them by the mission to last for a long time. After the meal Jimmie was very quiet. Suddenly he rose, puzzled. "Mother, do you suppose those people up in the nice and pretty homes know of Jesus?"

"Of course, James."

"But how can they? They never told us. Maybe they don't know. I'll tell them." And before his mother could stop him, he had pulled on his cap and rushed out into the blizzard.

Fighting bravely against the fierce wind and stinging snow, the lad made his way up the hill and across the streets to the big white houses on the hill crest. A lady gazed curiously at the ragged waif who had rung her doorbell.

"Missus," he ventured, removing his cap, "do you know Jesus?" Too astonished to answer, the woman only stared at the boy.

"What is it, wife?" A man appeared behind the woman.

"Did you ever hear about Jesus?" the lad repeated.

"Of course, sonny. Better come in and get warm before you freeze to death," the man said as he pushed the door open. Jimmie looked inside. He could see the glowing fireplace and feel the inviting warmth, but he shook his head.

"No, sir. If you know, then I must tell others." On and on he sped from house to house, always asking the same question and invariably receiving a "Yes" reply. At last he came to a house much larger than the others and much more beautiful. A man with an annoyed countenance opened the door and Jimmie asked his question.

"Have you ever heard of Jesus?"

"Yes" was the short reply. And the man was about to close the door in Jimmie's face when the persistent child leaned forward and asked the question that had been troubling his heart ever since he had been on the hill: "Then why didn't you tell us down in Tin Can Valley?"

"Why-er-er," the man stammered. Then, noting the shivering form before him—his countenance softened. Throwing his arm around Jimmie, he said, "Come in, son, and we'll talk it over while you get warm."

"Oh, no, sir! I have to tell others. Jesus told all who know about him to tell others. I must obey him. Thank you, mister," and he tore himself free and darted out into the snow.

Recovering from his astonishment, the man ran down the steps. But the deepening twilight and blinding snow hid the boy from his sight. He was unable to determine which way the lad had taken. "He can't go far," he muttered. "He is almost frozen to death now." Plunging into the blizzard, he pressed forward. Finding no trace of him, he at length ventured to a door and rang the bell. "Has a little boy been here recently?"

"About half an hour ago," the lady who answered the door explained. "And I have been worried over him ever since he left. He will surely freeze."

Murmuring a hasty "Thank you," the man retraced his steps and rushed on. Finally he saw a small figure ahead crumpled in the snow. He ran forward. It was the little missionary. "My boy," he said, grasping his shoulders and pulling him up.

"Don't stop me, mister," he answered, "I must go—on—tell—others." He swayed, and would have fallen, but strong arms were about him. The cold was too much for the thinly clad form. Rushing him into the nearest house, the man summoned a doctor while others rendered first aid. But it was too late. Jimmie's work was done.

The result? The wealthy homes were stirred. Hearts previously cold and indifferent were melted. Jimmie had given his life so that they might know Jesus—and to know Him is loving Him and others.

The inhabitants of Tin Can Valley were provided with more habitable dwellings, the men were given work and helped to get a good foothold in life. The Hollow was cleaned up and made beautiful, and at the very top of the slope, a church was built whose steeple reached toward heaven. Over the pulpit were written these words: "If you know Jesus—why don't you tell others?" placed there by the man who built the church and encouraged and directed the work done in the Hollow—the man who found Jimmie . . . or should I say: the man who Jimmie found.

IF YOU KNOW JESUS—WHY DON'T YOU TELL OTHERS?

WITH A STAR

ON TOP

....

Margaret E. Sangster, Jr.

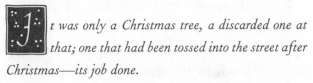 *t was only a Christmas tree, a discarded one at that; one that had been tossed into the street after Christmas—its job done.*

But not . . . quite . . . done. Thanks to that tired little tree, a miracle would take place.

(Late in the last century and halfway into this, there was no more loved name in inspirational storyhood than

Margaret E. Sangster. Then, as the years passed, this grandmother/granddaughter team was almost forgotten. But, here and there, there were those who preserved their faded and tattered stories. Now, a century later, a new generation is falling in love with them all over again; with stories like "The Littlest Orphan and the Christ Baby" and "Lonely Tree" (included in Doubleday's Christmas in My Heart® *series). "With a Star on Top" is so rare that, in a lifetime of searching for Sangster stories, I have found but one copy—and typewritten, at that.*

....

aybe we were so dragged out because we didn't have enough air in our flat. It was a railroad flat: four rooms, counting the kitchen. And all of us, Mama and Papa and the six kids, ate and slept and lived in it. There was one window in the kitchen, which was in the rear of the flat, but it looked out on a dreary court. The sun never penetrated into that court. In winter, the cold was like a shroud; and in summer, the most courageous breeze died of sheer discouragement before it got down to our level. There were no windows at all in the two middle rooms, but there was a window in the parlor in the front of the flat. It was a bay window that hung pre-cariously over a slum street.

A parlor? Yes. Mama insisted on having one, even though it was a drab, ugly room furnished with a sofa, sway-backed because of the sagging springs, and a couple of chairs, which hadn't any seats in them, and a table with a cracked marble top—Mama'd picked it up in a thrift shop. We kids used to beg for permission to sleep in the parlor, especially during the summer months when it was a couple of degrees cooler than the other rooms. But much as we begged, Mama never gave in. As she put it: "My folks always had a parlor, and I'm always going to have a parlor, too, as long as I live! No, you kids can't sleep in it. If we start sleeping in the parlor, we've lost our last grain of pride!"

Our last grain of pride, that's the way Mom put it! But how can you have any pride at all when you're per-petually weary, when your stomach is so empty that your soul's hanging by a thread? Papa was an itinerant worker. Sometimes he'd bring home a day's wage and drop it in Mama's aproned lap, and her eyes would cloud over. She'd finger the worn bills and the dingy coins, and we'd know she was translating them into something we needed desperately, not something we wanted.

She seemed to push herself around, Mama did. She was never cross to us kids. She seldom raised her voice to us, not even when we needed a scolding. But we felt, deep inside, that it was because she didn't have the energy to scold. It would have been an added effort at the end of a bad day, or the beginning of one.

Papa didn't scold, either—and I can't remember a single spanking that he administered. When he was home nights, he'd slump into a chair in the kitchen and stare into space. And if he spoke, which he seldom did, we kids would listen with both ears, because it was such a novelty. Although he'd come to America from Greece as a little boy, he still had a burr of accent. It seemed to thicken when he told us about the land of his birth.

"Blue skies," he told us, "and the blue sea, curling up against the shore. White sand, and trees everywhere, with glossy green leaves."

None of us had ever seen a tree with glossy green leaves. There was a little park about two squares away, just an area fenced off by rusty iron bars, with a flowerbed that never had any flowers in it, and five iron benches, and a tree. But the tree was a wizened thing that was afraid to put out foliage in the spring, scared of its own quivering shadow.

Sometimes, on a sultry night, I'd lie on the floor and look up at the ceiling and close my eyes, and I'd translate the traffic sounds that flooded through our flat into the murmur of the blue sea, curling against the silver shore. And instead of the dark ceiling, I'd imagine a network of branches with glossy green leaves. I guess the other kids used to imagine the same thing. That's why, perhaps, our tree was so important to us. For it was important to us in a way that none of you can imagine. You see the story I'm telling you is the story of a tree—a Christmas tree.

It had been an especially thin year for us. Spring faded, and summer was born and died, and autumn crept toward winter. The week before Thanksgiving we saw turkeys in the market, but we were too apathetic to long for one of our own. Christmas drew closer, with a drift of snow, but the white flakes that fell in our slum street were dirty even before they touched the ground. And yet, because kids and Christmas go together, because of the mysterious bond between them, we felt a sense of almost furtive excitement. Even though we knew there wasn't any Santa Claus with a pack of gifts swung across his shoulder, and that, if there had been a Santa Claus, he wouldn't have found his way to our flat, anyhow, we talked in whispers.

Mama, who had been born in this country, had warned us never to hang up our stockings. "It won't do any good," she'd told us. "It would just be one more disappointment."

But even so, we'd peer into store windows, with their glittering Christmas decorations, and when we came to the window with the toys, we'd stand with our noses pressed against the plate glass until they were flat, like white buttons. And in school, when they gave us Christmas songs, we learned them with the rest and sang them with the rest. "Jingle Bells," "Silent Night," and "O Little Town of Bethlehem." We weren't nearly so dragged out when we were singing.

Christmas came and went, as Thanksgiving had before it, with nothing special in the way of food or presents. But we hadn't expected anything special in the way of food, and neither had we expected any presents. We kids didn't have to go to school during the week between Christmas and New Year's, but it was freezing outside, so we huddled in the kitchen, close together, and waited for it to be night so we could go to bed. And then, toward the end of that long dreadful in-between week, Papa came home one night with a surprise. We heard a door open, below stairs; we heard his voice muttering in Greek, and then we heard a strange thumping sound.

Mom's face whitened and she said: "Your Papa must be sick: hear the way he's coming up the stairs." And she rushed to the kitchen door, which opened into the hall, and threw it wide. And there was Papa, and he was pulling something after him, and it was a Christmas tree. A Christmas tree that somebody had thrown out prematurely because they were tired of it, I guess. Papa didn't say anything. He just hoisted it over the sill and stood it upright in the kitchen, for it still had a platform, made of wood, attached to its base. And we kids came alive suddenly, and spread out until we made a ring around the tree, and our eyes and mouths were round O's in our faces.

And Mama's face was incredulous, and frightened. "Where did you get it?" she asked. "Where? Tell me."

Papa said, "I was shoveling snow on a street not far from Lake Shore Drive, and it was lying in the gutter. See"— his burr of accent had deepened—"there's still a star on top of it! The points of the star are a little bent, but"—he shrugged—"the star's bright, like real silver. And they didn't take off all the tinsel. There's still some of it tangled in the branches."

I was the oldest of the kids. I rushed to the defense of the star, even though a star needs no defense. I felt it was my duty.

"I don't think any of the points are bent," I said. "It's just the way the light strikes them, Papa, that makes them look bent." And my littlest sister whispered, "Is tinsel that shiny stuff?"

"Yes, the shiny stuff is tinsel."

And then suddenly Mama spoke vehemently: "How could people put a tree in the gutter?" she said. "What's wrong with people who would do a thing like that? It's beautiful, Papa. It's a beautiful tree!" All at once she was crying. "It's the first beautiful thing that's ever come into this flat," she said.

Papa's face was suddenly younger, and the bitterness that lived in his eyes faded out, ever so slightly. He said, "Every baby that's come into this flat has been beautiful." And Mama nodded and dabbed at her eyes with the corner of her apron.

And after a long moment she spoke: "We'll put it in the parlor," she said. "The kitchen's no place for a Christmas tree!"

And so, with us kids helping, we carried the tree through our windowless sleeping rooms and into the parlor. And once again, Papa stood it upright and there it was, with glossy green needles and a bent silver star on top and bits of tinsel clinging to its branches. And all at once my biggest sister, who was next in age to me, was unwinding the narrow red ribbon that was braided into her hair. And she took it over to the tree and dropped it on one of the branches and it made a spot of color against the green. And I knew that it was the only hair ribbon she owned, and it was as if she had offered up a sacrifice to the God who created Christmas trees.

There were two more days before New Year's: three more days of vacation from school. But now that there was a tree we kids didn't huddle in the kitchen anymore, we stayed in the parlor. And we cut strings of dolls out of newspaper and hung them in the tree. And Joe, who had the store on the corner (Joe was Greek like Papa), gave us a handful of cranberries, and we strung them and made a necklace for the tree. I found a piece of tin foil in an ash can and I blew the ashes away from it and rubbed it with a scrap of rag until it was clean. And we covered corks with the tin foil and they looked almost like Christmas bells. And suddenly the tree was alive with color and excitement.

And at night, when Papa came home from shoveling

snow or doing other odd jobs, he wouldn't sit slumped in a chair in the kitchen, he'd come into the parlor. And whenever Mama had a free minute, she'd creep into the parlor and crouch in front of the tree, and her face, when she raised it to the star, was the face of a middle-aged Madonna.

It was on New Year's Eve that Papa said, suddenly, "No reason why the springs should sag in the couch, no reason why it can't be mended." And we all waited breathlessly, because Papa'd never before suggested mending anything in our flat. We didn't quite believe that he'd go through with it. But the next day he got a hammer and nails and, with a potato sack that Joe at the corner had given him, he put a new bottom on the sofa and it didn't sag anymore because now the springs were held firmly. And I suppose that was the beginning of— well, call it our renaissance. No, it wasn't either. The beginning was that moment when Papa dragged the Christmas tree up the stairs and into the flat.

....

ew Year's Day was over and another week began, and it was time to go back to school.

We'd always gone to school reluctantly. We'd felt our-
selves inferior to the other kids, though we didn't put
our feelings into concrete words, or even thoughts. But
now we didn't feel inferior. We had a Christmas tree in
our house! When it came time for us to recite, we re-
cited quickly. And when the teachers asked questions,
we answered them correctly. And the teachers smiled at
us, because we were on our way to getting good grades.
They didn't know that we'd figured something out. If
we studied, if we gave correct answers, we wouldn't be
kept after school! And if we weren't kept after school,
we could go home sooner, to the tree. For it still stood
in our parlor, although the holidays were over.

And one afternoon when we came home, we found
Papa there, talking to Mama. He was saying: "It's crazy
for a strong man like me to be content with a day's work
now and then, when he can get it. That factory on the
south side, the new one, they've advertised many times,
and I bet I could get a steady job."

And Mama said, simply, "I bet you could"—and
then she hesitated for a moment and added—"dear."
And we'd never heard her call Papa "dear" before.

And from then on, Papa didn't bring home a little
fistful of money every so often. He brought home an en-

velope on each Friday night. And when he gave her the first envelope, Mama went into the parlor and touched the tree gently with one finger. And it was the way she'd touch the cheek of a new baby. For she was always gentle with a new baby.

And after Papa'd brought home four envelopes in succession we went downtown on a Saturday afternoon, all of us, and each kid had a new pair of shoes, and Papa had new shoes, and Mama had a new dress. And we came home, everyone carrying his or her parcel, but we didn't open the parcels in the kitchen, we opened them in the parlor in the shadow of the tree. And the next day, which was Sunday, the whole family went to church, the new shoes squeaking in unison as we walked down the aisle. And the squeaks sounded prettier than the organ music, which came later. And when we went home to dinner we had stewed chickens, two of them.

But when I asked Mama if I could eat my share in the shadow of the tree, she snapped at me: "No," she said, "the tree's in the parlor, and my kids aren't going to sleep in the parlor and they aren't going to eat in it."

And Papa grinned at her and he said, "Know what I'm going to do after dinner? I'm going to start putting new seats in the chairs. It don't make sense to have chairs that you can't use."

It was February now, and the littlest ones, who were in kindergarten, made valentines: red hearts cut from glazed paper. But they didn't send their valentines to anybody. They brought their hearts home and fastened them to the tree. The tree was so full of color, now, what with the things we'd picked up from here and there, that you scarcely noticed that most of the needles were gone, that the branches were brown and bare underneath. So what if they were brown and bare? When, at night, we lay staring at the ceiling, it was easier to see the network of glossy green leaves, and to hear the sound of the blue surf on the silver sand, because the symbol of Christmas still stood in our parlor.

Papa continued to bring envelopes home, one every Friday. And things began to appear in our flat that had never been there before. We no longer felt the ache of hunger, we were no longer so tired. When Mama sent us on errands, we ran both ways, and Mama, herself, walked with a lilt to her step. And once I heard her singing as she stirred something on the stove. And I stopped short and stared and she, feeling my eyes on her, turned and flushed and her song broke off, as if she were ashamed of it. But I knew she wasn't ashamed!

The tree was no longer a novelty. It was more than that. It was a fixture. It was an incentive. It was no longer a Christmas tree. It was our special Christmas tree. And the spirit of Christmas still lived in the star: the spirit of loving and giving! The Sunday Papa painted the parlor walls a soft shade of green, we danced around the tree and sang the "Jingle Bell" song that we'd learned in school, months before. And the new chair seats blinked at us, and when we flopped down on the sofa, breathless, at the end of the dance, it didn't give way beneath our combined weights. And I think the happiest day of my life, up to then, was the day that Mama led me shyly to the closet in the room where she slept with Papa and the youngest kids and pointed to three new dresses that hung from wire hangers. Never had she owned three dresses, at the same time.

....

Time went on and we progressed—but slowly. Because reformation and growth are slow when there are six children and two adopts to be considered.

Isn't it enough to say that our hands and faces were cleaner? That our shoes didn't get old so fast because we kept polishing them? And that our voices were kinder when we spoke to one another? And that Mama always kissed Papa when he brought home his envelope, and sometimes in the middle of the week, too?

And then it was spring, and though the tree in the park, two squares away, was afraid to put out new foliage, our tree stood in the parlor, staunch and tall and beautiful. And then school was over, and every one of us was promoted to the next class, and when we showed our report cards to Mama she kissed us, one by one, beginning with the littlest and ending with me. And there was a light in her eyes that told us how glad she was, although she didn't put her gladness into words.

And then the Fourth of July came and Papa took us to the beach—all of us, except Mama, who didn't feel like going to the beach because the seventh child would be coming almost any day. She said she'd feel easier sitting in the parlor, with the tree. And when we came home in the dusk and climbed the stairs, we were tired, but not dragged-out tired—happy tired. But our happiness melted away into little puddles when we heard Mama crying in the distance. Papa growled something under his breath—and

it might have been a prayer and it might have been a pro-
fanity—and he hurried through the flat, with all of us
trailing after him. And there was Mama, huddled in the
parlor—and the tree was gone! And when Papa thundered
out a question, she told him what happened.

"A policeman came," she sobbed, "and took it away
with him. He—he said it was a fire hazard because it was
so dead and old and the branches were dry and brittle,
and there was so much junk on it—that's what he said.
He took our tree, and I've cried until I have no tears
left."

....

ll at once we children were bunched together in
the old way. And I found myself thinking, *It's all
over! Papa won't have a job anymore, and there won't be
envelopes every Friday, and we won't have new shoes. And
Mama's dresses will get soiled and shabby, and there
won't be enough food, and we'll be dragged out, again.
And the springs will begin to come through the bottom of
the sofa.*

And then suddenly Papa's voice rang through the

desecrated parlor and broke through my ugly thoughts. And what he said I shall always remember:

"This is the day of the country's independence," he said. "It is the day when men decided that they should be free, and as they wished to. Sure, they have taken our tree away from us, but they cannot take away what the tree stood for. They cannot take away what it has done. Look, you kids"—he was shouting, now—"we're going away from this flat, this slum, this city! There are farmers who need men to work for them in places where there are many trees. And if a man works hard enough, he may someday own his own piece of land, and the trees that grow from his own soil will belong to him. And no one can take them without his consent!"

Once, the thought of moving away from a place where we had always lived would have terrified Mama. But in those days, Mama had been bogged down by weariness. Well, she was bogged down now, after a fashion, for she was carrying a new life within her. But she scrambled to her feet, clumsily, and went to stand beside Papa, and his arm circled her shoulders and they looked brave and eager.

And she said simply, "May we go soon, darling—?"

She'd never called Papa "darling" before, only "dear" occasionally. "I should like," she added, "for the new baby to be born in the country, where there are many trees."

And that was the beginning of a way of life that we had never known existed. And every time I see an evergreen, standing strong and straight and coming to a point like an arrow of the Almighty on its way to heaven—every time I see a tree trimmed with tinsel and colored balls with a star on top, I'm back in a dingy parlor with a bay window looking out on a slum street, and I'm young again and feeling my first thrill of hope.

So this is the story of our Christmas tree. And it's a story that has lasted all the way from then to now, just as the tree has lasted.

MERRY "LITTLE CHRISTMAS"

Agnes Sligh Turnbull

S ibling rivalry. All it takes is two children—and you have it. But what if one of them is beautiful, charismatic, multitalented, a born leader, and a scholar of the first rank? And one of them is none of the above. What does a mother do? What if a mother never did . . . and now it is too late, for both are now grown? . . . And, *just as bad, her son is in danger of choosing the wrong woman, the wrong values.*

She was filled with foreboding, this Twelfth Night, the so-called "Little Christmas," for it appeared that the family was crumbling around her.

What on earth could she do?

(Agnes Sligh Turnbull [1888–1958], author of bestsellers such as The Crown of Glory, The Bishop's Mantle, *and* The Golden Journey, *wrote of a world where values were crucial. Critics might accuse her of a lack of realism, but she always maintained that her books and stories mirrored the gentler world she grew up in—a world she felt had much to teach us in our frantic-paced society. The fact that she is still read half a century later is proof that she may have been closer to the mark than were some of her cynical critics.*

This particular story made mere kindling of my emotional defense system and strode right into my heart. Just as this book was going to press, I found for the first time the complete text, making it even more powerful. I submit that this is one of the ten greatest Christmas stories ever written.)

....

argaret Greaves gave a last wave from the front steps as Henry's taxi lurched off down the icy street, then, shivering, closed the door and moved dispiritedly toward the living room.

Christmas was over again, with all the so-called festive season, and she had never before felt quite so weary in body and mind, or so completely frustrated in heart.

This year, as always, she had looked forward to the great occasion with almost childish eagerness. Hank coming home from the university, Penny from college, Cecily and Bill, her husband, out from the city, the family together again and, pervading all, that beautiful, delicate thrill of happiness which had been a part of Christmas in the past!

But it hadn't worked. It never did, now; only this year everything had been worse than usual.

Margaret sank down on the divan and looked about her. The room had the cheerless, untidy look which falls upon a house at the end of the holidays. *If this were only all,* she thought! *If a good day's cleaning would set everything right, how simple it would be.* But the trouble went much deeper.

Even so, she knew that the best immediate ease for

the worries and disappointment of her heart was work. Penny's room upstairs was still in a whirlwind state after her departure yesterday, and Hank's not much better after his leaving two days before. At least this business trip of Henry's, while it left her lonely, would give her a chance to clean up.

She looked at the faded holly, the mistletoe, and the small tree. She would begin with them, for this was the day to take them down. It was Twelfth Night. It was also Epiphany, or "Little Christmas," as old Anya, who had lived with them when the children were small, had always called it.

Suddenly a soft, startled flush rose in Margaret's cheeks. She sat there, thinking, and then she spoke aloud.

"Little Christmas!" she repeated over and over. "Little Christmas, now, today, and mine if I want it!"

And she knew that she *did* want it! More than anything else in the world, she craved a second chance this year at keeping Christmas. Then, like an excited girl, she began to plan. First, she would make the living room clean and shining. She would take down the withered holly and substitute fresh greens; remove (with what a feeling of relief!) the absurd glass unicorns and golden balls that Cecily had arranged upon the mantel; she would even bring down from the attic the old creche and the figures of the Shepherds and the Wise Men, which in the past had been the mantel decoration each Christmas.

Margaret remembered now the first time that Cecily had found fault with them. It was her first Christmas home from college.

"Mother, do we *have* to have all that old rubbish again on the mantel? It's all so frightfully old-fashioned. I'd love to try something original. Something *startling*."

....

As usual they had given in to Cecily, and the effect had been startling enough. It was the following year that she begged to trim the tree herself.

"I've got the most marvelous idea, Mother! It seems awfully childish to keep on hanging up the same old baubles. Do let me try out my idea. Please!"

Of course they had let her. It would have been hard to refuse her anything that Christmas. She had come home president of her class, with four A's on her report and a special commendatory letter from the dean. She was also to have the lead in the sophomore play and had had a painting in the college art exhibit!

But that was Cecily—beautiful, brilliant, incredible. Beauty and brains, with artistic gifts added, had made her always the center of every scene.

When young Hank had been born, the fact that he was a boy had balanced the fact of his more or less ordinary features. And as he grew older, he had held his own with sturdy masculine normality.

It was Penny, their third child, who had been the problem. Her hair was dark and straight, her eyes shy and gray, her features too strong to be pretty. In school her work was not even quite average. Somehow she was always falling behind. She couldn't make one of the biggest colleges, certainly not Cecily's, but she finally managed to enter a smaller one.

Margaret recalled again that first year that Cecily had taken over the trimming of the tree. For some reason she had not connected it before, but she realized now that it had been on that Christmas that Penny had been so *very* difficult. Henry had been annoyed to the point of sharpness, and Margaret herself had been mystified and hurt.

Now, suddenly, she wondered if it *could* have been on account of the tree? Penny had always been the one to bring down the ornaments from the attic and had always insisted upon climbing the ladder to fasten the star on top.

Margaret eyed the small fir upon the table, decked in skillfully devised paper rosettes, behind which all the tiny lights showed purple. It was, one had to admit, artistic and original, but it did not look like Christmas. Margaret went over to it now, almost wrathfully. She took off the rosettes and put them in the wastebasket. She put away the lights, then lifted the tree and threw it out the back door.

Once started upon her work, it was amazing how rapidly it went. She went to the attic for the boxes which contained the creche and figures. Then, slowly and tenderly, she arranged them as they always used to be.

She stood back and surveyed the room. It was beautiful! Tonight she would light the candles, and have a fire, and do all the things she always wanted to do at Christmas. Perhaps in the very doing of them she might find some sort of refreshment and wisdom to take up again tomorrow the cares that lay upon her heart.

She glanced toward the corner where the big tree had always stood. It was silly for her to want it there again tonight, but she did.

If she could but have it, clothed in its old ornaments, with the toys underneath which the children had always placed there, it would be like reliving those happy days when Christmas had been pure joy.

Margaret thought intently. Next door lived the Dyers. Their children were small and their tree was large. She did not delay, lest reason and decorum should overcome her. She caught up a coat and went next door. Little Mrs. Dyer was just dismantling the tree.

"Are you planning to do anything with it?" Margaret asked after the first amenities were passed.

"It's a problem, isn't it?" Mrs. Dyer said. "I think I'll just throw it out in the backyard for the present."

"Would you give it to me?" Margaret tried to be casual. "You see, I've a silly notion to try a little experiment in decorating—before another Christmas, you know—and our tree this year is too small to work on."

It didn't sound *too* fantastic as she had put it, Margaret hoped. Mrs. Dyer agreed with relief.

....

argaret thought of her young neighbor as she went back home. She was the kind of girl she hoped Hank would marry someday. So bright and gay and modern, yet such a fine mother and homemaker. Would Hank choose wisely? Would he wait until he really knew what he wanted?

This girl he had taken out during the holidays was so pert, so sure of herself, so ultrasophisticated. Her eyes looked hard and calculating and there was a brittle note in her laughter.

It worried Margaret terribly. Hank hadn't gone all out for a girl before. He had always "played the field," as the boys called it. Now what if the superficial glitter of this girl had really caught him? And she was all wrong for him, Margaret knew instinctively.

Above everything else, she had always prayed that her children might have happiness and lifelong contentment with their loves, as she and Henry had had. At this point her heart seemed to turn over twice as she thought of Cecily and Bill, for that, of course, was the most acute pain.

She was scarcely home, before the oldest Dyer boy brought in the tree. She did not hurry. Indeed she loitered as she trimmed it, stopping often to hold the oldest baubles in her hand. The fruit, for instance—the red apple, the golden peach, the bright green pear. The children had particularly loved these for some reason. There was the little silver trumpet, too, and the pink wax rose, the bluebird, and the angel. These, also, had had special significance.

At last there was nothing left but the star that went on the very top. She thought of Penny, who had always begged to hang the star.

Penny, their strange, inscrutable daughter, who was flunking two subjects this first semester!

She just didn't seem to care. When she got home they had discussed it earnestly with her, but as usual could get nothing out of her. She had only mentioned casually that she had broken a swimming record. This, to Henry, had been the last straw.

"A swimming record!" He had all but yelled it. "Do you think we're paying fifteen hundred dollars a year for you to go *swimming*? Now, this nonsense has to stop; you've got to get down to work."

Penny had said nothing, and gone up to her room. And now, what if she really flunked out of college? What was to be *done* about Penny?

She had always been dependable in other ways. Cecily often forgot things. It was Penny, silent and un-demonstrative, who was always there when needed.

It was Penny's gift which had pleased her mother most of all this year, a tiny bottle of the rare flower perfume which Margaret loved. It must have eaten a big hole in Penny's allowance! It was plainly wrapped, with a small card bearing the words: "Merry Christmas to Mom from Penny."

Cecily's gift had been a bizarre green handbag which did not go with any single costume Margaret possessed. It was tied with yards of silver and gold ribbon, and the card read: "Oceans of love to the most wonderful mother in the world."

Margaret sighed. Before long we would know about Cecily and Bill. They had told her of what threatened, each in characteristic fashion.

"Mother, I can't believe it! It's simply *too* marvelous!" Cecily had begun when they were alone for a few minutes the day before Christmas.

Margaret was used to this introduction. It meant that some new success had come to Cecily.

"What is it, dear?" she asked eagerly.

"I've been offered the position of associate editor on the magazine!"

"Why, Cecily! Oh, that's wonderful! Darling, I'm so proud of you!"

"What's up now?" Penny had inquired, coming into the room.

Margaret had repeated the news and Penny, without comment, had passed on.

Cecily continued: "Nobody knows how I've wished for this job! How I'll love it! And I know I can make a go of it, only . . ."

"Only what?"

"Bill is being absolutely mulish about it."

"What do you mean?"

"Well, we had decided that I'd take time off this coming year to have a baby. With the new job I can't. I think Bill ought to be reasonable. There's plenty of time." Cecily's lovely face had suddenly stiffened. A new note had come into her voice. "I might as well tell you that this may be serious between us. He's just about issued an ultimatum, and nobody can do that to me."

"But darling, surely you can compromise somehow." She realized now, ashamed, that her immediate reaction had been that Cecily must not be thwarted in this, her crowning honor.

Cecily had turned away. "Maybe you can do something with him," she said, and all at once her voice sounded flat and tired. "You know he always listens to you."

Bill had followed her up to her room that night, where she was frantically wrapping the last packages. She had had such a hectic day, and even now the turkey stuffing had to be made before she slept. She loved Bill, and because he had no mother of his own, he had somehow taken her to his heart.

"We're in trouble, Mom, Cecily and I. It's bad."

"Oh, Bill, she told me. You *mustn't* let anything spoil your marriage. You must try to see each other's side of things."

"I needn't tell you how I love Cecily. You know that. But she's got to decide now what she wants."

"Bill, dear, she's young yet. She could take time off later . . ."

"Some girls could, but not Cecily. I know her even better than you. In a few years this magazine thing will be a tremendous job. There will never be any time in Cecily's life for having children and making a home for them. As a matter of fact," he added slowly, "there may not even be much place for me, if she goes ahead."

"Bill, don't say that."

"I'm only facing facts. But one thing, Mom, you've got to believe. It's Cecily's happiness I'm thinking of, too, and not just my own. I've seen plenty of lonesome career women of forty-five."

"So have I."

"That's why I'm fighting with all I've got for both of us."

She had kissed him with her eyes full. "All I want is for you both to be happy. But try your best to understand each other. I'll tell Cecily the same. And let me know as soon as it's all settled."

Margaret gave a physical motion now of shaking the anxiety from her. No word had come from them yet. Whether the omen was good or ill, she did not know. She hurried through her solitary dinnner, and then lighted the logs in the fireplace. Then she lit the candles, snapped on the button which illuminated the tree, and sat down, a sense of peace stealing over her.

This one night was all hers in which to make up for what she had missed, and gird herself for all that was to come. She suddenly knew that the one of her children who would most enjoy this with her would be Penny. Even though she would say little, she would like it.

"I broke a swimming record . . ." The sentence

flashed into her mind. Those were the words that Penny had injected casually the day they had talked with her about her work. And except for Henry's flare-up, they had passed the information by without comment, in their concern over her studies!

She had broken a record. What record? They hadn't even asked.

All at once Margaret sat very straight. That had meant a lot to Penny. She had been laying her triumph before them in her own way, and they had ignored it.

She saw it now with sudden insight: this was the very first triumph Penny had ever had. She had always loved to swim, but nobody had thought much about it. But now *she had broken a record!*

Margaret rose with instant decision, went to the telephone, and called Penny long distance.

"Hello, dear." Margaret knew she sounded nervous.

"Hi, Mom. Anything wrong?"

"Not a thing. Penny, I want to know about that record you broke in swimming."

"You *what?*"

"Tell me all about it. Penny, please. What record was it?"

"Well"—she could hear the faint note of pleasure

that crept into Penny's voice—"you see the college here doesn't compete. We just have our own team. But of course we keep track of the records. And just before Christmas I busted the hundred-yard freestyle American Women's Intercollegiate!" She hurried through the words, but her mother could feel her excitement.

"Penny! Why, that's simply tremendous! Weren't they thrilled at school?"

"Oh, they made sort of a fuss."

"Darling, I'm so proud of you I don't know what to do!"

There was a dead silence on the other end of the phone. Margaret went on. "I wish you were here tonight. I'm all alone, you know, so I'm celebrating what Anya used to call 'Little Christmas.' Remember? I'm having everything just the way we used to when you were children. The creche and the figures are on the mantel, and I borrowed the Dyers' tree and put all the old trimmings on it."

"Mom, you *did?*" Her words were quick, incredulous.

"Yes. Does it seem too crazy?"

"Is the bluebird on . . . and the rose?"

"Yes."

"And the *fruit?*"

"Everything."

"The peach was mine. I was always afraid Cecily would want it, but she picked the apple. The pear was Hank's. You . . . you didn't bring the toys down, too, I suppose?"

"Yes, I did. The doll and the bear and the dog. They always had to be there. This year things were not just right. I wonder whether you know that Cecily and Bill . . ."

"Cecily's a fool. If I had as nice a husband as Bill, I'd *want* to have his children."

"I'm sure you would, dear. I wish Cecily were more like you."

There was another breathless second of silence, and then came a strange, husky voice.

"Would . . . would you say that again?"

"I said," Margaret repeated distinctly, "that I wished Cecily were more like you."

"Mom . . ."

"Yes, dear."

"I'm awfully glad you called."

"So am I."

"Are you going to call Hank?"

"I hadn't thought of it."

"I believe he'd like to hear about the tree. And Mom, tell Dad I'll make up the work. It won't be too much trouble. I . . . I sort of feel different now, somehow. Sort of . . . happy!"

"I'll tell him, darling. Lots of love. Goodbye."

Margaret sat at the desk, her eyes wet. So many things seemed clear now. She put in the call for Hank. She doubted whether he would be greatly interested, but it would be good to hear his voice. When she told him rather apologetically what she had done, Hank didn't laugh.

"Have you got the trumpet on the tree?" he asked.

"Absolutely."

"And the pear?"

"Yes."

"I remember how I always liked those best of any-thing. I had to fight Cecily for the trumpet, but I stuck it out."

"I brought the old toys down, too. You know, the favorites that you children always thought should enjoy Christmas with you."

"You did? Say, you're going sentimental in a big way, aren't you, Mom? I remember how Penny used to sneak them down and hide them behind the tree when we'd really outgrown them. Penny's a good kid."

"Yes, she certainly is," Margaret agreed, with a catch in her throat. She told him about the swimming record. Hank was excited.

"No! Honest? Broke the hundred-yard freestyle? Why, that's big-time stuff, Mom. She never said a word."

"Write and congratulate her, Hank."

"You bet I will. Why, that's really tops. You know, Penny has a lot on the ball. Well, what else are you doing tonight, Mom, all by yourself?"

"Oh, just the things I didn't have time to do on the real Christmas. I like old-fashioned customs, just"—she hesitated—"just as I like some old-fashioned qualities in girls."

"Yeah, I guess I do myself, when you come right down to it."

"They're likely to wear better in the long run, Hank."

"You can say *that* again!" There was a faint edge in his voice.

(*He's beginning to find that girl out,* Margaret thought. *He's going to be safe after all.*)

"Mom, I sort of like picturing the room the way it

87

was when we were kids. Let's have it like that next year."

"We're going to. And now, good luck, dear. Good-bye."

Margaret went slowly back to the couch and sat down, a warm glow in her heart. Now for the evening. She had collected the selections she liked best of the seasonal literature. They were on the table beside her. They ranged from "The Night Before Christmas" to the Gospel according to St. Luke.

She smiled as she fingered the books. No matter if there were contrasts among her favorites, she would read them just the same. She would also play some carols.

"Mother and her everlasting carols!" Cecily used to say. "Don't you ever get tired of them?"

She put a fresh log on the fire and sat down again with a deep sigh of contentment. Even as she did so, there was a quick tap-tap on the knocker and then the opening of the front door. She knew at once that it must be Cecily and Bill. Cecily came into the room, her face white and set. Bill followed her, looking as though he hadn't slept for a week. Margaret knew what they had come to tell her. Now, tonight, this night!

But they were both looking around the room in amazement.

"Well, what on earth!" Cecily cried.

"This is Twelfth Night," Margaret said. " 'Little Christmas.' I wasn't satisfied with our Christmas this year, so I'm celebrating it again. I'm going right ahead with my plans, even though you are here."

Bill was over at the mantel, looking at the creche and the figures.

Cecily was at the tree. Her mother couldn't see her face, but she saw her touching the various ornaments.

"Where's the apple?" she asked.

"Up there, higher, to the right."

"It and the angel were always mine," she said.

"What was that?" Bill asked.

"Nothing," said Cecily. Then she gave a quick exclamation.

"My heavens, you even brought down the old toys!"

Bill was beside her now, peering under the shadow of the tree. Cecily picked up the doll, but suddenly put it down and turned away, as though she had been guilty of folly.

Margaret spoke firmly. "I am now about to play and

sing some carols, and then read some Christmas selections. I ought to warn you."

Bill went over to the fireside chair and sank into it. His face under the table light was haggard and drawn. Cecily glanced quickly at him, then sat down on the couch. Her beautiful profile was still cold and bitterly set.

"I suppose we can take it," she said.

Margaret played and sang from memory, trying by a tremendous effort to think of the familiar words and not allow herself to break down under the impact of the misery which hung over Cecily and Bill.

She moved from one old favorite to another, and at last she came to "Silent Night." As she sang, her heart all but broke in yearning over her children, sitting in the same room with her and yet so far away.

Bill was leaning forward now, his head in his hands; Cecily was sitting motionless, her eyes upon the tree. Once her mother saw her look at Bill and then glance quickly away.

Margaret rose and came back to her place. She tried to speak brightly.

"Now," she said, "I'm going to read my old favorites. You can still escape if you want to."

Neither spoke, so she began. She read "The Night

Before Christmas." When she finished, she looked musingly at the burning logs.

"When the children were small, Bill, we always let them help trim the tree the afternoon before Christmas. Then, after an early supper, they came down in their pajamas and bathrobes and sat on the rug before the fire while I read them this poem. Do you remember, Cecily?"

"Of course," she said in an odd voice.

Margaret picked up the next book. "Then, when they grew older, they still liked this Christmas Eve ritual, only we added bits from *A Christmas Carol*. They loved the Cratchits best of all."

As she read from the worn book with its familiar markings, she glanced up once or twice to look at the haggard young man and the stony-faced young woman. She found their eyes on each other, Bill's anguished and beeseeching, his wife's—but she couldn't see into Cecily's.

Something of the humble happiness of the Cratchits seemed to be released from the pages, and hover about the room.

"Do you remember how you children always worried about Tiny Tim's fate each year, even though you knew he wasn't going to die?"

"I remember," said Cecily.

Margaret's throat felt tight.

"And now," she said, "I'm going to read the sweetest story of them all."

She picked up the small black book beside her. Her voice was low, and she read slowly.

And it came to pass in those days that there went out a decree from Caesar Augustus that all the world should be taxed.

As she went on, she felt the weight of her own emotion overcoming her. Margaret knew she would never finish the chapter.

And she brought forth her firstborn son, and wrapped him in swaddling clothes and laid him in a manger; because there was no room for them in the inn.

Her voice caught. She closed the book and laid it back on the table. Silence filled the room. She was afraid to look up as the moments passed.

Then at last she sensed that Cecily had risen and

gone over to Bill. Margaret raised her eyes then and saw her standing there, her cheeks wet with tears, her face bearing upon it the tender portent of the woman she would one day become.

"We've got to go, Mother. Bill's awfully tired. He ought to get some rest. It's been wonderful being here tonight. And, Mother, put the toys away carefully. You can't tell what may happen before another year!"

....

When they had left, Margaret came back into the pine-scented, fire-warmed, candlelit room, her heart melting with joy! New wisdom and understanding had come to her along with hope and relief. On this, the anniversary of the holy night when the Wise Men had come to worship the baby in the manger, her own children had been given back to her, safe from the perils which threatened them.

They were all one now, as in the past, close and secure in the circle of love. If only Henry were here to rejoice with her, it would be complete.

She raised her head, thinking. She couldn't bear to have him shut out of the strange and wonderful happiness of this night. She could not telephone him, for this was the evening of the big banquet. But she could send him a wire!

A little smile played over her lips as she mentally framed it. She could picture Henry receiving it when he came back late to the hotel. He would be first startled, then, as he read, puzzled. At last he would tuck it into his inner pocket with that familiar, half-quizzical, half-adoring expression in his eyes. He would be thinking, *What's she been up to now?*

Margaret repeated the message three times before the operator got it:

"Merry Little Christmas, and all my love."

THE INVISIBLE

CHRISTMAS TREES

William Barthel

he lights had finally "come on again . . . all over the world" . . . and the men and women who had made it through the long, bloody war were "home for Christmas."

But Bob Stevens wanted more—he wanted to give his mother and sisters presents. So here he was in bustling

New York City in a battered old truck, full of Maine Christmas trees.

But before he could even get started . . . both the truck and the trees had been stolen.

What could he possibly do now? What he did . . . and the enigmatic young woman who provided the inspiration . . . represent the rest of this remarkable Christmas story, first carried by The Reader's Digest *thirty years later.*

....

few days after the Thanksgiving of 1945, my wife's Uncle Bob Stevens bundled 230 Christmas trees into an old truck and headed from Maine to New York City to make his fortune. That was the way he put it, but what he meant was he wanted to earn enough money to give his mother and three sisters a very merry Christmas—the first peacetime one in four years. His father had died at sea early in the war, and Bob had spent the previous Christmas in a woods near Bastogne, in the Battle of the Bulge.

He reached New York on a dark and windy afternoon. As he drove up and down the avenues, what he noticed most was all the fir trees nodding to his fir trees from street corners, storefronts, and parking lots. It seemed that a great many people were out to make their fortunes selling Christmas trees that year.

It was dusk when he arrived, by chance, in Greenwich Village. He parked, and tucking a large, flat parcel under his arm, began wandering through the meandering streets with their colorful shops and lively people. Down one narrow street he discovered a small Italian delicatessen, brightly lit, with a narrow concrete patio in front that was probably used for outdoor tables in summer. It would be a great place to sell trees.

Inside, the air was warm and fragrant. Salamis, sausages, cheeses hung in festive rows above the counter. Holiday cookies filled a glass case, and crusty breads were piled in straw baskets. Bob inhaled and grinned and stated his business, offering Old Joe, the owner, a percentage on every tree sold.

Old Joe conferred with Young Joe and Mamma, a solemn woman in a black dress and white apron who regarded Bob with a mixture of suspicion and curiosity about the package under his arm.

"Let me show you my sign," Bob said. He tore away the wrapping to reveal a homemade wooden panel with CHRISTMAS TREES FOR SALE in shiny red and green letters.

But Bob hadn't stopped at that. The sign was filled to overflowing with exuberant scenes of a New England Christmas. Carolers and shoppers strolled between the letters. The O in FOR was a skating pond alive with children. There was a snowy barn with a Christmas tree on the roof, a horse-drawn sleigh ride, a church. On the left of the sign it was Christmas Eve, on the right Christmas Morning. At the top, Santa and all his reindeer rode the moonlit sky. Bob had created an American Primitive, touched with innocence and joy.

Young Joe and Mamma were smiling when Old Joe held out his hand to Bob. "You will sell your Christmas trees here," he said.

Bob left his sign with Old Joe and went back to where he'd parked the truck, tired but happy. But there was only a bough in the gutter at his feet. The truck was gone!

Somebody directed him to the police station on Charles Street. The sergeant on duty didn't seem at all surprised to hear about a stolen truck full of Christmas trees.

"Now that might qualify as perishable cargo," he said. "I sure hope you find them before Christmas, because you don't get much call for them after."

Bob thought the sergeant had the pronoun wrong.

He was hoping *they* were going to find them. "Shouldn't be so hard to locate an old truck with a Maine license, loaded with Christmas trees," he said.

"Fourth of July, maybe, but right now—figure it out, buddy."

Bob had only a few dollars in his pocket, and the bank had loaned him the money to buy the trees. He had a bad night's sleep in a rooming house and went back to the police station early in the morning. No luck.

He walked glumly to the store and saw the two Joes hanging the sign outside on the patio. Soon they were draping a string of Christmas lights along the top and sides. It looked terrific.

When Old Joe heard the story, he patted Bob's shoulder and took Young Joe inside. Bob was still staring at the sign. He had no idea that something right out of O. Henry was about to happen to him.

It was only nine o'clock in the morning, but down the street came a dapper gentleman, walking very slowly, taking time to avoid objects in his path which he alone could see. He was already tipsy at that early hour, and at his heel was a limousine driven by an anxious chauffeur. The man saw Bob's Christmas tree sign. He read it carefully and turned to regard the empty patio.

"Best Christmas trees I ever saw," he said. "Can't beat 'em."

The man kept staring. "Wonderful trees," he said. "Can't make up my mind. I'll take them all."

The chauffeur had stopped the car and was holding the rear door open. "Burton," the man said, "put those trees in the back." Then he turned to Bob and put something in his jacket pocket. "That should cover it," he said.

In spite of his troubles, Bob laughed as the car pulled away. Then he put his hand in his pocket and felt a crumpled ball of paper. It was a $20 bill. It was against Bob's nature to get something for nothing. He ran to the corner, but the limousine was already out of sight.

When he returned to the sign, a tall, dark-haired girl was studying it intently. Her cheeks were colored by the cold and her eyes were smiling.

"Did you paint this?" she asked. Bob nodded. "It's marvelous. But where are the Christmas trees?"

"Just sold every last one of 'em." Bob found himself telling her what had happened. "I guess I can afford to wait around another day or so," he said, "but then I'll have to take a bus home."

"Oh, don't *quit*. You don't have to stop selling Christmas trees just because you haven't got any!"

The girl was hurrying away. "Wait," Bob called after her. "My name's Bob. What's yours?"

She looked back with a laugh. "You may not believe me, but my name is Holly." She disappeared around the corner, leaving Bob to wonder what her words meant. You don't have to stop selling Christmas trees just because . . .

Bob bounded into the store. "Hey, Joe, would a town like this have a lumber yard?"

There was a lumber yard on East 12th Street. Bob spent most of the $20 getting a hundred pieces of clear pine cut on a jigsaw. They were six inches tall.

He bought brushes and quick-drying paints at an art store and worked all day and most of the night. The next morning he had Christmas trees for sale, all "trimmed" in his primitive style—with tiny ornaments and candy canes, toy drums and horns, Christmas stars and angels.

Old Joe brought the outdoor tables up from the cellar, and Mamma covered them with bright-green cloths to display Bob's trees. He sold them for stocking stuffers, ornaments, table decorations, and he used the profits for supplies to make new trees. And he kept looking for the girl.

He didn't see her again until the middle of December. She came by in a rush, her arms full of books, even prettier than before. She looked at Bob's trees and flashed him the V for Victory sign. "They're wonderful, Bob. Now personalize them."

"What?"

"Just decorate one side. Paint the other a pretty color, but leave it blank. Then you can put a girl's or boy's name on it—or anybody's—to order."

"Say," Bob laughed, "who are you anyway?"

"Just a schoolgirl." She told him the name of the university she was attending and then was gone before he could ask her address.

The personalized Christmas trees were even more popular than the others. What everybody liked best, though, was the Christmas tree sign. Several people wanted to buy it, and the owner of an art gallery on Eighth Street offered him $75 for it. Bob said he'd sure think about that. He began taking the sign to his room at night, saying he wanted to work on it some more.

The day before Christmas Eve, Bob got a present from the New York City Police Department. They'd found his truck behind a deserted warehouse in Brooklyn. The trees were gone, but nothing had happened to the truck. There was even a half a tank of gas.

It was time to head home. Bob personalized trees for

Old Joe and Young Joe and Mamma. Then he settled up accounts.

"What about the sign, Bob?" Old Joe said. "You take it over to Eighth Street, and you got yourself seventy-five bucks."

Bob took the sign down and polished it lightly with his sleeve. *My luck*, he thought.

"It's the end of an era," a voice said behind him.

"Holly! I was just going to give this to Joe to keep for you—I knew you'd be by." He turned the sign over and handed it to her. "I personalized it," he said.

On the back of the sign was the word HOLLY, surrounded by pictures of a dark-haired girl celebrating Christmas in New York. She dashed in and out of the letters with her arms full of presents. She ran up to a sidewalk Santa, bustled into a Village toy shop, hurried past the tree in Rockefeller Center. She was off on a dozen holiday errands, East Side, West Side, all around the town.

"I'll love it all my life, Bob."

"Holly, let's have lunch before I go." He saw her hesitate and knew she was expected somewhere. "You know how you always look?" he said. "You always look like you're double-parked."

"All right, wise guy. Just let me make a phone call."

They had lunch in a restaurant owned by Old Joe's cousin, a Christmas feast complete with wine. Bob told Holly a little about the war, how it was good being back home in Maine. But jobs were scarce, and he had no idea what he was going to do with the rest of his life.

"What would you be," Holly asked, "if you could be anything?"

Bob hesitated. "I spent some time at the Battalion Aid Station," he said. "Nothing serious. I was what you called 'walking wounded,' and a doctor commandeered me to assist him. He worked for a stretch of sixty hours before he keeled over. If I could be anything . . ."

Holly leaned across the table and touched his arm. "You certainly have the hands for it," she said. Then her eyes flashed fire. "Well, don't think you can't do it just because you don't think you can do it!" It was another of her curious pronouncements, and the words were already stuck in his mind.

Bob spent the rest of the day Christmas shopping, then headed home, his truck a Santa's sleigh. The family celebrated Christmas for days. When Bob stopped in at the bank to repay his loan and open a savings account for $216, the bank president was impressed. He asked Bob his future plans, and the words spilled out as Bob told him how much he wanted to go back to New York to medical school. That night, the banker talked with two other citizens of the town. Some long-term loans were offered to supplement Bob's G.I. benefits.

It turned out to be a great investment for Maine. Today, thirty years later, my wife's Uncle Bob Stevens is a Maine doctor in the old-fashioned sense of the word, working too many days and nights. But he still finds time for painting, and his style remains deceptively simple and clear.

Some of his most treasured paintings are of weddings and receptions. All of Bob's sisters are married, and at reunions they tease him because he has just the right touch of gray at the temples, and because his tailor-made clothes hang so well on his lanky frame. Sometimes Bob's mother joins in the kidding, saying he'll soon be setting up practice on Park Avenue.

The truth is, Bob does look as if he's been a distinguished doctor all his life. If I said he was once a penniless painter selling Christmas trees in Greenwich Village, I don't know who'd believe him.

Except my wife's Aunt Holly.

A CHRISTMAS
MIRACLE

....

Kathleen R. Ruckman

Many have written in urging me to include this moving story in one of my collections. It is easy for us to be smug because of incredible advances in medical science. Yet deadly diseases akin to the diphtheria of this story still come at us—diseases which are usually fatal and for which there is no known cure. Suddenly, within mere hours, the homes have emptied their children *to fill newly dug graves in the icy graveyard. How could Christmas possibly coexist with such tragedy?*

That was the question.

The author, now living in Oregon, wrote me about how the story came to her: "I remember my grandmother, Suzanna, telling me and my sisters and cousins this story many times since I was a child. We would sit around the kitchen table as she told stories. Because I am a freelance writer, I was the one who wrote her stories down."

....

I t was December 23, 1908, and a plague of diphtheria swept through eastern Czechoslovakia that Christmas season. In the tiny village of Velký Slavkov, lying in the shadow of the High Tatra Mountains, a solitary man walked a deserted street. Pushing his hat lower on his head against the bitter wind, the man pressed ahead, passing homes with drawn shades and tightly shuttered windows.

For weeks, diphtheria—an acute infectious disease that strikes the upper respiratory system—had ravaged the small towns along the foothills of the Tatra region. Nearly half the townspeople of Velký Slavkov had fallen to the plague; many of the victims were young children less than ten years of age.

Carrying a pail of black paint, the man climbed a flight of outdoor stairs and swabbed an X on the wooden doorpost of the Boratko household. Another home was quarantined.

After the man left, Suzanna Boratko kneeled at her doorpost, weeping and praying in Slovak. In less than a week, she and her husband, Jano, were suddenly childless. Their oldest child, five-year-old Mariena, had succumbed to the disease a few days earlier. In the backyard, Jano labored in the woodshed, pounding the last nail into a coffin he was building for his two sons, who had died earlier that day from diphtheria. Between sobs, Jano coughed and wheezed, because he, too, had contracted the deadly plague.

Suzanna returned to the house. Crying in agony, she cleaned and wrapped her sons for a final time, carefully laying them into the handmade pine caskets. She and Jano lifted them onto the wagon, and with a quick jerk of the reins, started the slow journey to the town cemetery.

Driving the horses through the foot-high snow, Jano and Suzanna braced themselves against a chilling wind that stung both body and soul.

"Another trip to the graveyard is more than I can bear!" Suzanna cried out as they passed house after house marred with the black death mark. The couple empathized with those families, but they didn't have the strength to offer sympathy or encouragement. They were too wrapped up in their own grief, much like the cotton muslins tightly swathed around their sons.

Two more gravesites had been dug into the frozen earth. Now, all three children were together for eternity. Suzanna, struggling through the Lord's Prayer, hugged the cold ground and wouldn't let go. Jano finally pulled her away with what little strength he had and led her back to the wagon. She clutched her empty arms and crossed them over her broken heart. She reminded herself that she would never hold her babies again.

Tomorrow was Christmas Eve. As Jano and Suzanna reentered their barren and branded house, they needed comfort. They needed solace from their village friends. But no one dared come near. There were no Christmas greetings. No sympathies were extended. The black X spelled DEATH and DO NOT ENTER. Their dark house was a frightful, forbidden tomb.

Little high-laced brown leather shoes were still lined up against the wood stove—as they usually were when the children were tenderly tucked into the same bed. But now, the large feather bed was empty, and the old stucco house had never felt so cold.

"I won't see another Christmas," Jano whispered weakly to his wife. "I don't think I'll see the New Year in, either."

He pushed away the soup and bread that he could not swallow. It was as though the diphtheria had tied a noose tightly around his throat, neither allowing food nor sufficient air to sustain him. The village doctor had shrugged his shoulders when he visited Jano a few days before. He had no cure.

Suzanna gathered some kindling wood and lit a fire for the night, sure that her husband was about to die. Morning arrived—Jano was still alive. Snowflakes fell from a gray sky and the wind blew a white mist over the frosted windows. Suzanna, exhausted from a restless night with little sleep, dipped her cloth again in cold water to cool Jano's burning fever. Then, rubbing the icy glaze off her lattice window, she fixed her eyes on the Tatra Mountains. Her mind contemplated Psalm 121: 1-2: "I will look to the hills from whence cometh my help."

Suddenly, her gaze was interrupted as she saw a peasant woman trudging through the snow. The old woman's red and purple plaid shawl, draped over her hunched shoulders, hardly seemed warm enough against the morning chill. A babushka, or kerchief, was wrapped around her head. Her long peasant skirt was a bright display of cotton and linen patchwork, and her woolen leggings and high-buttoned boots allowed her to successfully trod the snow-filled street. In one of her uncovered hands she held a jar of clear liquid. Suzanna stood half-stunned as she watched the old woman shuffle up the forbidden walkway.

Suzanna heard the knocker strike twice. She cautiously opened the door and saw an unusual face, one wrinkled from years of farmwork and severe winters. But her eyes expressed a warmth that filled Suzanna's heart.

"We have the plague in our home, and my husband is in a fever right now," Suzanna warned her.

The old woman nodded, and then asked if she could step inside. She held out her little jar to Suzanna.

"Take a clean, white linen and wrap it around your finger," she instructed. "Dip your finger into this pure kerosene oil and swab out your husband's throat, and then have him swallow a tablespoon of the oil. This should cause him to vomit the deadly mucus. Otherwise, he will surely suffocate. I will pray for you and your family."

The old woman squeezed Suzanna's hand and quickly stepped out to the frigid outdoors. Never before had Suzanna's heart been touched in this way. Here was a poor woman appearing—in love—on her doorstep in the midst of a plague. Her unexpected gift was a folk remedy against diphtheria.

"I'll try it," she called out to the old woman, with tears in her eyes. "God bless you!"

Early Christmas morning, Jano retched up the deadly phlegm. His fever was broken. Suzanna wept and praised God. A flicker of hope lightened her heart for a moment; surely God would someday bless her and Jano with more children.

There were no presents under a trimmed and tinseled tree that Christmas morning. But the jar of oil glimmering on the windowsill was a gift of life for generations to come.

POSTSCRIPT: In the days following the miraculous healing of Jano, Suzanna shared the folk remedy with her neighbors. In the 1920s, Jano emigrated to America to find work. Suzanna joined him later with their nine children.

Their ship reached Ellis Island on Washington's birthday, February 22, 1926, and the family settled near the steel mills of Johnstown, Pennsylvania. The family consisted of a set of triplets, two sets of twins, and two single births. Two of the triplet boys were named John and Paul, after the two sons who died from diphtheria. The other triplet was named Samuel, who today is the father of this author.